The RAGGLY SCRAGGLY NO-SOAP NO-SCRUB GIRL

By David F. Birchman ◇ Illustrated by Guy Porfirio

Lothrop, Lee & Shepard Books   New York

What I remember most about that summer is the dust.
Each day it came looking for us children, and each day it found us.
We didn't mind it one bit. But Mother, who did not tumble, roll, or
romp about in it, fought the dust with a fury. She scooted it out the
door with her broom, beat it out of her rugs and blankets, rubbed it
off her tables and chairs, and scrubbed it off her children.

Every Saturday night after dinner, Mother rolled up her sleeves and came after us with a vengeance. "Get down the tub, Father!" she shouted. "And bring in some firewood. It's high time we scrubbed all these raggly scraggly children!"

Father put the tub on the back porch. Then Mother poured steaming water into it, and we shed our week-worn clothes in a heap at the porch door. She bathed the babies toes to toes and the rest of us knees to knees. The floor of the porch became slippery with lye soap and water while we jostled each other to be next in line to squeal and splash under Mother's washcloth. Finally she toweled us dry, put us into fresh pajamas, and tucked us into bed.

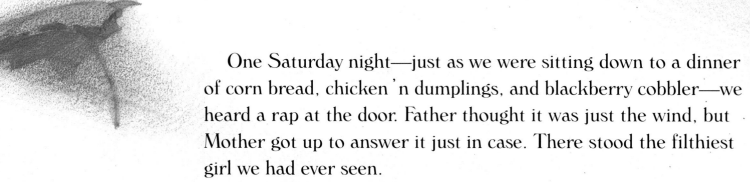

One Saturday night—just as we were sitting down to a dinner
of corn bread, chicken 'n dumplings, and blackberry cobbler—we
heard a rap at the door. Father thought it was just the wind, but
Mother got up to answer it just in case. There stood the filthiest
girl we had ever seen.

"Good evenin', all," she said. "I'm the Raggly Scraggly No-Soap
No-Scrub Girl, and I've come to gobble up your food and grease up
your plates."

Mother looked over the rims of her glasses at the strange little
dust-covered creature standing before her. She seemed puzzled,
but Mother was not the kind of person to question a hungry guest,
so she tucked her bewilderment inside her bandanna and welcomed
the stranger in.

By the time the girl reached the table, we were already hard into dinner. The clicking and clanking of forks, spoons, and knives filled the air. But sooner or later, each of us surfaced long enough to gawk at the dinner guest.

"Never mind guardin' your grub," said the Raggly Scraggly No-Soap No-Scrub Girl. "I can't say that I'm extra special hungry this evenin', unless you're havin' corn bread, chicken 'n dumplings, and blackberry cobbler." Then she reached down the neck of her coat and drew out a gigantic soup spoon. She licked the spoon twice and dug right into the chicken 'n dumplings.

Watching that girl eat was a humbling experience. In one hand
she held a great slab of corn bread, which she used to sponge up
the dumpling gravy. Once it was full, she swallowed it in a gulp.
The other hand, the hand holding the gigantic spoon? Well, that
one moved just too dang fast for us to tell.

"When are we gettin' to the blackberry cobbler?" she asked as
she polished off the main course.

Mother studied her for a long painful moment. She was just about to raise a scolding finger when Father suddenly threw up his arms.

A huge raven had flown in the window and was trying to land on his shoulder. It tottered there briefly, flapping its dusty wings, then hopped onto the table—smack-dab into the blackberry cobbler.

"Well, look at this!" exclaimed the Raggly Scraggly No-Soap No-Scrub Girl. "Snitch has come to visit, too."

"Snitch is high stepping cobbler all over the dinner table!" yelled Mother. "Shoo him out of here this instant."

"I would, ma'am," said the girl, "but he doesn't shoo easy."

"I'm not asking you to shoo him out easy," replied Mother. "I'm telling you to shoo him out *now!* "

"Shoo, Snitch," hollered the girl, waving her arms. "Shoo! Git! Shoo!"

The raven cocked one eye and then the other. Then it picked up the cobbler pan in its beak and, using the length of the table as a runway, launched itself into the air. As the raven circled the room, chunks of cobbler dropped everywhere. We children hid under the table, but the Raggly Scraggly No-Soap No-Scrub Girl just sat there, catching falling crumbs on her tongue. Finally the bird dropped the pan, right side up, into her dusty lap and glided out through the window.

"Thanks lots, Snitch!" called the girl, and she crammed what was left of that cobbler into her mouth with both hands.

Mother sat unmoving in her chair, glaring at our dinner guest. She was all frowned up and about to thunder. But Father quickly pulled out his harmonica, tossed it over to me, and yelled, "Play us a tune, Zachariah. Play us a tune for dancing. Play us a tune for buckling up the floor!"

Father picked up little Ansonia and waltzed her once around the room. Then he pulled Mother up out of her chair.

"Now you just stop this," she protested, but she was smiling. All around the floor my parents danced—stepping gingerly over the cobbler, sliding every so slightly through the blackberry juice.

When they were all out of waltz, Father and Mother collapsed in laughter onto the sofa. Mother fanned herself with her apron. "Please close the window, Zach," she panted. "We've got a swirl of dust blowing around."

"That's no swirl of dust," I said. "That's the Raggly Scraggly No-Soap No-Scrub Girl!"

The girl whipped around the room faster than dancers can dance or crows can fly. All you could see of her was a blur of dust. It wasn't exactly a dance, but it was amazing. I let the harmonica fall from my hands and stared. We all stared.

"She's got almost as much talent for dancing as she has for eating!" I exclaimed.

Then the spinning girl became visible again and collapsed on the sofa between Mother and Father. "It's been a long time since I've used my dancin' feet," she said, "and it's been a long time since I've had a meal quite this fine. I'm much obliged to you. But eatin' and dancin' sure do take it out of a body. Think I'll close my eyes for a spell."

"You do that, child," said Mother. "You just rest yourself."

In a blink, that Raggly Scraggly No-Soap No-Scrub Girl was asleep and snoring. She snored while the table was cleared and the room was mopped. She snored when Father brought the old tub to the back porch and fetched the firewood. She snored while the tub was filled and all of us squealing children were scrubbed and dried. She snored until Mother said, "It's high time we scrubbed this raggly scraggly girl. She needs a bath."

The girl's eyes popped open. "Bath? Bath! Noooooooo, ma'am! I don't take to baths and baths don't take to me! I'm the Raggly Scraggly No-Soap No-Scrub Girl. I'm a dancer in the dust. I'm all of me dirt, and none of me clean."

"Come now, girl," Mother said. "A bath will do you wonders."

"I already got more wonders now than I know what to do with, ma'am," said the girl. "A bath wouldn't do me no good, leastwise not enough good to undo the bad it would do me." She edged toward the door. "Think I'll be leavin' now. Thank you, folks, for havin' me."

Mother looked at her sternly and shook her head. "I just can't let any child leave my house looking as filthy as you do." She slipped between the girl and the door. "Get yourself ready for a bath."

A look of fear came to the Raggly Scraggly No-Soap No-Scrub Girl's face—not simple ho-hum fear, not "I'm sort of scared" fear, but sheer, stark terror. Suddenly she turned and bolted from the room.

We all bolted right after her, chasing her
from one room to the next. She yanked
doors open and slammed them behind her. As
fast as we ran, she was always one slamming
door ahead of us. In a single minute, she
circled the entire house and exploded onto
the back porch, leaving the screen door
twisting on one loose hinge.

There was no way that anyone could have stopped her had she not placed her foot squarely down on that cake of lye soap. But step on it she did, and before we knew what was happening, she flipped forward right into the tub.

She landed with an enormous SPLASH! Then her body sank into the suds so that all you could see was the top of her head.

For a long moment, everything was still except for a strange gurgle troubling the surface of the water. Then the girl surfaced in a fury, spitting and clawing and churning up the water. She sank again as quickly as she had surfaced.

Mother rolled up her sleeves to pull her out, but suddenly she popped up on her own, flew through Mother's arms, scrambled over her head, and hightailed it out into the darkness. "My, oh my!" exclaimed Mother. "I've never seen a child take so poorly to a bath!"

That old tub of ours was never the same after the Raggly
Scraggly No-Soap No-Scrub Girl fell into it. Try as she might,
Mother just couldn't scrub it clean. Steaming bath water would
turn muddy brown before we even stepped in it.

Mother had to admit she was licked. She planted dusty millers
in the old tub and sent Father into town to buy a bright, new, shiny,
galvanized metal tub that held twice as much bath water and twice
as many raggly scraggly children.

I have no idea what became of that Raggly Scraggly No-Soap
No-Scrub Girl. Who knows where a girl like that gets to when she
makes up her mind to get herself gone? But you know, the dust
always comes again after the rain, and a dirt-covered child always
comes along on the heels of a freshly scrubbed one. So maybe, just
maybe, she'll be back. After all, Mother makes mighty fine corn
bread, chicken 'n dumplings, and blackberry cobbler.

To Genevieve, my raggly scraggly girl
D.F.B.

To my lovely wife, Gabriela
G.P.

The illustrations in this book were done in watercolor paints and colored pencil. The display type was set in Burlington and Script MT.
The text was set in Windsor Light. Production supervision by Esilda Kerr.
Text copyright © 1995 by David F. Birchman
Illustrations copyright © 1995 by Guy Porfirio
Printed in the United States of America
First Edition 2 3 4 5 6 7 8 9 10
Library of Congress Cataloging in Publication Data
Birchman, David Francis. The raggly scraggly no-soap no-scrub girl / by David F. Birchman: illustrated by Guy Porfirio.
p.   cm. Summary: Although she may be able to keep her house and her own children clean, Mother is no match
for the dusty dervish that shows up one Saturday night.
ISBN 0-688-11060-6. — ISBN 0-688-11061-4 (lib. bdg.)
[1. Cleanliness—Fiction. 2. Baths—Fiction.] 1. Porfirio, Guy, ill. II. Title. PZ7.B511817Rag 1995 [E]—dc20
92-40339 CIP AC